PROFESSOR & ROBIN

Case of the Golden Mint

D.H. WALTERS

Little Free Library

Take a book; leave a book
littlefreelibrary.org

PRESS

Edited by Xulon Press

ISBN 9781498460330

www.xulonpress.com

Wait for the Lord:
Be strong and take heart
And wait for the Lord.
Psalm 27:14 NIV

PROFESSOR KLULESS & Robin
In

The Case of the Golden Mint

Chapter 1

It was a cool September night as Robin was walking home from school past "THE YARD." She had stayed late for the first week of her senior year of high school to try out for one of the many sports programs. Athletics were not her gift but she was terribly lonely—too lonely for a seventeen year old. She was trying to find a way to fit in and make friends. She was like a lot of kids who weren't real popular, she spent time with her computer and music; listening to romantic songs and dreaming of the days she would spend with her truest friend. Her computer was a real gamer too; she had been given her choice of a cell phone or gaming computer. She chose the computer because she didn't have many friends to talk to anyway.

"THE YARD" was a beautiful place this time of year. The leaves were turning colors, with bright red and yellow hues. "THE YARD" had been the most beautiful estate in the area before it was deeded over to the city for back taxes. It was then taken over by city employees, including the police department. As she passed "THE YARD," she greeted one of her few friends; Dutch, the keeper of "THE YARD." He was a magnificent animal for a middle-aged German Shepherd and was respected by all. He loved the attention, but he wasn't approachable by many people. Her next stop was inside "THE YARD" to visit Professor Klueless, a man of 80+ years and quite absentminded. He was allowed to help around "THE YARD," although Fredrick Standridge, the manager, was officially in charge - right after Dutch that is. The Professor was very intelligent, but with his advancing years, he had become hard to live with and even harder to understand. He had no other place to spend his time, either. After a while he would just get on people's nerves. He had been an important man on the police force, and gained wide

respect for his ability to close difficult cases. If he started to reminisce,
his stories could go on for hours. Robin
was trying to act important around the
Professor, hoping to feed her desire to
be needed and move from an acquaintance
to a real friend; but the Professor was
self-absorbed and normally in his own
little world.

Just as she was about to leave a
small fleet of cars came in for decommis-
sioning. For some unknown reason, the
Professor got up from his corner desk
to inspect them before they were sent
to salvage. He looked in the trunks,
checked under the seats and spent a lot
of time in the glove compartments. He
was in and out of each of them quickly
until he got to the last car. Robin
wanted to say goodnight, so she went
over to see what the old guy was doing.
As she arrived, she could see him just
sitting on the passenger's side seat
and looking at an item he had removed
from the glove box. He was just sitting
there, staring at something as if he
couldn't quite figure out what it was.

Robin yelled as she hurried over,
"What did you find?" He didn't answer.
As Robin approached, she could see that
the Professor was holding a scrap of
paper with some printing and a partial

map on it. He lifted himself up and squinted over the driver's dash and wrote the car's ID number on the back of the note. "What is it?" She asked with great enthusiasm. The Professor still didn't respond. He was staring at the paper and mumbling about having to stop them, whoever they were. He then pulled himself out of the car and hurried back toward his desk. Speaking to himself, he was mumbling about trying to trace the note. As he dialed the phone and began a conversation with the local authorities; Robin pulled her laptop from her back pack, peered around the Professor's head to read the number and typed it into the search engine.

Professor Klueless wrote the word "stolen" on the note while Robin located the previous owner's information from Carfax. "Professor, I've got the owner's name and phone number right here." He pushed her gently aside and quietly spoke, "I'm sorry. I don't have time for you now. Why don't you run along and I'll see you tomorrow, OK?"He wouldn't take no for an answer, so she grudgingly left, hanging her head in rejection. (I wish he would let me help, the computer can make mincemeat out of these tasks.)

She headed to the 5th Ave shoe store, her last stop before going home for another boring night. She was looking forward to seeing Josh; she always did. Josh was a young man of nineteen who worked at the 5th Ave shoe store. Robin would often dream about him at night. He was her best friend, although she was drawn to him romantically. Josh lived with his grandfather, who was quite old and didn't pay much attention to him. Josh's dad would sometimes come and live with them for a few months of the year and then just leave until about the same time the following year.

Josh saw her coming through the store window and smiled, inside and out. He looked forward to her coming, especially when business had slowed towards the end of the day. Selling shoes was not the career he had planned for himself and held little excitement for him. Robin was his best, and maybe only, friend. He ran to open the door for her and greeted her with his big smile.

"I'm so glad you could come today. I'm bored out of my mind," he exclaimed.

"My day wasn't exactly stellar either. The Professor discovered something in a decommissioned fleet car, but he wouldn't let me help him."

"What did he find?"

"It looked like a crazy map with some kind of message printed on a note with it."

"Did he give you any idea of what it said?"

"No, he just called in the vehicle number and told me to get lost until tomorrow. I think he mumbled that the car was stolen, but I'm not sure."

"If it was a fleet car, it probably didn't matter, but I'm curious to know more about the note."

"Well, maybe tomorrow I'll find out. Is there anything new at the store?"

"Nothing! We sold a few pair of shoes, but it was kind of a slow day. We did get a lady that bought five pairs of shoes. She does this once a month and then returns them in the next few weeks; maybe it's her life's excitement. Grandpa said that she has been doing this for years, but averages to only keep about one pair a month. I need to find a life."

"I know what you mean. Heard anything from your dad - isn't it about time for him to come home again for a while?"

"Haven't heard anything yet, but he usually comes in January, after the Christmas holidays are over. He comes all tired out, eats, uses the whirlpool, sleeps and by April he feels better and leaves. I've wanted to talk to him and grandpa about college, but I never seem to find the right time."

It was getting late, so after a brief hug, Robin started off toward home; another routine day came to an end. At least they had the beautiful weather to enjoy before winter set in. Tonight would be more of the same routine, supper, homework and another long night. Robin would lay in her bed for hours dreaming of what she wanted her life to be like; having good friends, a little excitement and of course Josh.

Chapter 2

Meanwhile, back at "THE YARD", the Professor was working extremely hard at trying to imagine all the possibilities to explain the note he had found. The map had no street markings and the brief printing was only a portion of the original, torn and burned. It carried the odor of cigar smoke, but that could have come from the driver, with no connection at all to the note. What intrigued the Professor was its heading, "The Day of Retribution" and a date of Oct 31st.

There were other words missing, but it clearly printed the word "mint." This was enough for him to assume that somewhere, at sometime, someone was going to get even for some bad tasting mint treats. It could be almost anything edible with a mint flavor. He had less than sixty days before Oct. 31st to prevent a total catastrophe. The Professor was sure that this person, or group of persons would try to put a poison of some kind into the treats to get even with for the bad tasting confections. In his days on the force, he ran into a lot of crazy people that went to great extents to satisfy their anger. He approached the puzzle like any analytical genius would:

1   He got out his collection of maps and began to look at the road patterns in the local area to try and find a match.
2   Then he would check every bakery in the area for any bad mint creations until he found the correct location for crime.
3   He then could check all the incoming ingredients until he found the poison. Just simple deductive reasoning.

He was very proud of this plan.

Before Robin knew it, the next boring school day had passed and she was in her everyday routine of walking home. The first stop was to see Dutch; it was the high point of his day. Dutch seemed to be able to tell time extremely well and always waited for her at the entrance to "THE YARD". He was never more than a few minutes off schedule.

Oh, how Robin wished he could talk; maybe about his experiences at "THE YARD", maybe about the secrets of "THE YARD", but at least he always brought her what she needed most -love. He didn't mind the attention either. Dutch had been more involved with people when the Professor and Fred were younger, now he just did his primary job of protecting "THE YARD". On long hot days, maybe he thought about the times he found drugs or a missing person, a rescue, or some other exciting event.

"Dutch, I'm so glad to see you today." Robin stroked the back of his head and played with his ears. He had a ticklish spot right in back of the right ear that she always seemed to find. "Anything new?" She asked him almost expecting him to answer. After a few minutes of greeting, Robin got back up to her feet and started to leave. "Sorry buddy, but I need to see if the Professor needs me."

Robin entered the room, gave Fred a quick hand signal to say hi, and walked to the Professor's desk. The Professor sat in his chair as in a trance, almost as if he hadn't moved all night. "Good afternoon Professor. Did you find out anything new?" Robin asked. The Professor didn't even move to acknowledge her presence.

"Professor, are you there?" Robin tried again. This was very frustrating to her.

Finally, he moved, "Oh, are you here again?"

"Did you find out anything new - I mean about the note?" Exclaimed Robin.

"No - not exactly, but I'm checking my maps. Where did I put those anyway?"

"What exactly are you looking for? Maybe I can help?" Robin said as she pulled out her laptop like a quick draw artist.

"I was looking for streets — yes, city streets, I think." The Professor said as he scratched his forehead.

Robin was already in MapQuest, "What city?"

"I'm not sure, but they have to have a bakery in it."

Robin went from excitement to, here we go again and closed her computer. The Professor continued, "I think we need to find a bakery, or maybe a candy factory that sold a batch of bad mint flavored confections. I figured some guy got a bad taste in his mouth and wants to get even. No telling how many people will get sick with a nut like that running around loose. It never used to be like this, people had respect for one another. I remember the time…."

Robin had already turned him off and began concentrating on the problem as she saw it. Just then she noticed the Professor getting up and walking toward the door. "Hey Fred, give me the keys for the truck or one of the old fleet cars," he said. Robin knew that was not a good idea. Last time he drove, "THE YARD" got over a dozen phone calls from angry motorists. I'm not sure putting "THE YARD"'s phone number on the vehicle was a good idea, she thought to herself. She could only imagine how many calls they would get if the message, *Tell me how I'm driving* was also written on the vehicle.

"No, I can't give you any keys! Do you remember what happened the last time you drove? You're not on the insurance anyway," Fred hollered back. "But how do you expect me to solve this case with no transportation? Besides, I was driving before you were born," the Professor responded. Fred thought to himself *there wasn't as much traffic with a horse and buggy, and besides you didn't need insurance back then.*

Robin motioned to Fred to throw her some keys, he did, and off they went. Robin had insurance through her family and Fred knew it. Robin's jaw almost hit the ground as she read the writing on the key, *Big Bertha*. Big Bertha was a small, over powered tow truck owned by "THE YARD" for emergencies. Maybe Fred was protecting them or thinking this was an emergency. The truck wasn't that hard to drive. It was a six speed automatic and fairly new, but still bigger to navigate then the compact cars of the day. Robin didn't even want to think about parking the beast.

"Robin, I didn't ask you to go," the Professor complained.

"If I don't go, you don't go," she relied as she slid into the driver's seat. "Where to?"

"A bakery? Any bakery?" Said the Professor. "It doesn't matter which one. We need to start somewhere."

Robin knew where a bakery was close to the school, so off she went. It really didn't matter to her where they were going, it beat being alone and bored. When they arrived after a quiet trip, Robin was thrilled to see that the parking lot wasn't crowded. The whole lot was empty so she could have as many parking places as she needed. Before the engine was turned off, the Professor was out the truck door and into the door of the "Campus Bakery." By the time she was out the truck door, he had already approached the counter and asked, "Do you have any bad tasting mint cookies, pies, or candy?"

The lady behind the counter rolled her eyes and said with a forced smile, "No sir, we only have great tasting goods here." As the Professor started back to the truck, totally satisfied with the answer; Robin approached the counter and explained the best she could. The sales lady smiled and explained that as far as she knew, no bakeries in the area had received an excessive number of complaints about anything lately. Robin thanked her and headed back to the truck. The Professor said, "Well, that's one down; to the next please." He then checked it off his list: Campus Bakery - OK.

Robin was relieved when she was able to convince the Professor to go back to "THE YARD". It was getting close to supper time and she hoped to stop to say hi to Josh. Seeing Josh would complete her day and she even had something to tell him. Driving with the Professor was a real experience.

Chapter 3

J osh was at the window and saw Robin coming down the block. He had been worried about her, she usually came an hour earlier.

"Robin, are you OK? I started to worry about you. It was getting late and I thought I may have to leave before you showed up."

"Sorry, I've been playing chauffer to the Professor. You'll never guess where we went."

"It can't be that bad," he stopped and waited for her to reply.

"You can't imagine what it's like to take the Professor someplace. We took the small tow truck and went to the Campus Bakery of all places. Then I had to smooth it over with the lady at the counter after he was rude to her."

"I can just see your face red as a beat and you talking really fast, 'Sorry about the old guy, he's nuts.'" Josh made funny faces as he talked and they both broke out into tremendous laughter. The harder they laughed, the funnier it sounded.

"I'm so glad to have you for a friend, you make everything better." She stared into his eyes, hoping to see him return the gesture. "How was your day?"

"Every day here seems the same. I feel like I need to get on with my life; I'm just wasting time here."

"I'm sorry you feel that way, Josh," Robin replied sharply, her feelings hurt.

"No, I didn't mean you. You're the best thing that has ever happened to me, but I need to get my life going. I can't sell shoes for the rest of it."

"I'm sorry too. I'm so afraid you're going to leave and I'll have no one."

"Don't worry Robin - you're my best friend. I'll always be here for you, promise."

"Have you ever talked to your dad or grandfather about your future?"

"Not really. Even though I've lived with Grandfather, I don't really know him. I know my dad even less. They have never spent time with me; they just give me food and shelter. I don't even know what my dad does for a living. The servants provide all my daily needs."

"I guess all we have is each other. I hope we never lose that." Robin said with a smile. Both of them just sat there looking at each other, not really knowing what to say, but happy just being together.

"Well, I guess I'll start for home. My parents won't be happy about my being late for supper or else I'll find it on the stove and they won't even notice." They got up and gave each other their usual quick hug and she was on her way.

As she walked, her mind began to dream of what she would really like; Josh to be more than just a good friend. She had never had a real boyfriend, but if it wasn't for Josh, she didn't want to live. The thought of him leaving, if just for college, would create a hole in her life that could never be filled.

Chapter 4

Another long day at school; it seemed like it would never end. Robin thought "How can all this stuff they teach be important in life? I can't understand it much less use it." She lived for the few hours between the end of school and her arrival at home.

As she passed the fenced area surrounding "THE YARD", Dutch was nowhere in sight. Normally, he was waiting for her and watched her approach. Robin buzzed at the gate call box and Fred opened the gate for her from his office. Instead of going into the admin building, she went into "THE YARD" to find Dutch.

The wall around "THE YARD" was made of brick with a black iron railing and provided a safe, but secure environment. The landscaping work, on the other hand, had declined over the years due to budget constraints. "THE YARD" was immense and no one knew for sure if Dutch had any favorite places. Robin listened intently for anything that would give his location away. Hopefully, Dutch wasn't sick or hurt so badly that he couldn't attract help.

Robin saw something move out of the corner of her eye. It looked like a small black ball of fur, maybe a baby skunk? She slowed her speed, not wanting to get into something that she was not prepared for. The ball of fur turned and yipped at her through the tall grass. Robin stopped dead in her tracks. It was a puppy, but where did it come from? It was so small and cute and so unexpected!

Then she caught a glimpse of it; the puppy was mostly black with a white spot on his back and small white boots. The race was on. The puppy was very young but, quick, slippery, and fast in the open range. The grass was so long, it seemed to hide it every few steps. Robin couldn't imagine where this puppy came from or where he was headed. The chase ended in the wood shed of an abandoned admin building. There was Dutch trying to keep up with six other puppies and no mom in sight. Dutch was beside himself. No one guessed he was a family man and he sure was not equipped to keep the kids out of trouble. Dutch came over to Robin and cried. His patience was exhausted.

"It's ok, Dutch. Where is the mom?" Robin asked as if she was going to get a verbal response.

The puppies were lively and in apparently good condition, but they were looking for some supper and Mom was nowhere to be found. Robin wasn't sure if she should pick up the puppies and bring them to Fred, or just leave them there and wait for the mom to return. One thing was certain; the puppies didn't care about her presence and were getting hungrier by the minute. I think Dutch was just glad to have help arrive and it looked as if he was ready to give the problem to Robin so he could get about his duties. The puppy that led her there seemed to bunch the others like a herding dog.

Robin began walking to the main building to tell of her discovery and get some help when she noticed the Professor searching in the fleet car where he had found the note. He was examining the cracks and crevices looking for clues, but he looked like a lost bear trapped in a garage bin with no room to maneuver. As usual, he was unaware of her coming.

"What are you looking for Professor?" she asked.

"I can't talk now. I'm trying to find something - anything that can give me a clue."

"Professor, I found Dutch."

He cut her off. "Can't talk now," he said as he raised his voice a little.

"But, Professor" Robin spoke, raising her voice a little as well.

"No buts about it. Can't you see child, I'm trying to save lives? I did find some crumbs that I'm going to analyze, but it may not mean anything at all. Why don't you go talk to Fred? Yah Fred."

Professor Klueless scraped some crumbs from the glove box and a few from the floor then started for his office. In the old equipment room there was a spectrophotometer which hadn't been used in years. A spectrophotometer is a device that, after being calibrated with a known sample, shows the characteristics by a spectrum of light. He didn't do a good job of keeping the crumbs separate, so it was hard to believe any real clues would be found. Not only did the Professor not remember how to work the device, he didn't have a recent sample to be used as a standard.

While the Professor was fiddling with the experiment of the day, Robin looked for Fred to report the addition of Dutch's family. Needless to say, Fred was not overjoyed like a new father. "This is a place of serious business, we don't have time or resources to play with animals."

"But you still need to do something with them," Robin restrained her reply.

"Ok, you take care of them. You can take them home if you want, or sell them but just get them out of here," he responded.

"I will, I will, but right now I think they're hungry," Robin replied with a grimace.

"Well go buy something. Here's some money from petty cash."

"Sir, a dollar won't buy them anything."

"I think we have some evaporated milk cans that are military surplus. You can use those."

"I need a way to give them the milk too," reported Robin.

"There is a new rubber glove in the closet, take that and see if it works."

Robin grabbed a few cans of the milk and one rubber glove and went off to try to feed the puppies. It was funny, now that the puppies were found; Dutch had no more interest in them. Robin prepared the glove for the puppies, filled it, and sat with the puppies smelling the food and climbing all over her. The glove had only five fingers and there were seven hungry puppies. The puppies were not considerate of each other, but competed to be fed. After five were finished and satisfied, the remaining shy two were fed. The shy two were more interested in being held than in eating. One was the puppy that led her there and acted like he was in change, the other was a little girl she would name Princess. She was so small and unable to compete with the boys. Robin took her time with the last two and then started back to the office, trying to decide on the way if the puppies should be moved and to where.

As she opened the office door, she could hear the Professor shout with his victory celebration, "I've got it, I've got it!"

"What did you find Professor?"

"I ran a test on the crumbs found in the car and discovered that they were from a donut. Now, we can narrow our search to donut shops. Maybe these bandits are corrupt policeman, they are the biggest eaters of donuts, you know. I'll get my map and check all the donut shops within sixty miles. "

Robin reached for her backpack, and located the computer to google donut shops in the area.

"No time for games now, I've got to get the phone book and check the yellow pages for donut shops."

Robin shut her laptop, put it back in her backpack and headed out the door. As hard as she tried, she didn't seem to fit in and no one wanted her help. Now her time with Josh was coming up, the part of the day she loved best. Soon the thoughts of where to find a home for the dogs were replaced by thoughts of Josh. Tomorrow, she would feed them again and maybe Fred will have found them a new home.

Chapter 5

As Robin walked toward the shoe store, her countenance brightened and thoughts of what she would tell Josh filled her mind. It was always a struggle to know what to say and when to listen, but she didn't want to offend the only friend she really ever had.

Maybe Dutch hadn't watched for her today, but Josh did. As much as it pleased him to see her come, it would disappoint her not to see him in the window watching. If the store ever had a busy closing, it would crush her terribly.

"Hi Robin, what stories do you have for me today?"

"They're not just stories, they're happenings."

"Ok, what's new?"

"How about - puppies?"

"Oh, did your parents get competition for me?"

"No, seems like Dutch has a private life." Robin said with a smile.

"I love to see you smile."

"You're probably the only one who does."

"So, what's the 411 on the puppies?"

"Actually, Dutch had to babysit them in "THE YARD" and we don't know who or where the mother is. I'm going to have to feed them until Fred finds them a home, all seven."

"Sounds like you're going to be late for a few days." Josh said with a frown.

"Maybe a little, but I'll get here as quick as I can. Have you heard anything from your father yet?"

"I heard a couple of servants talking about dad. They said that he is getting too old, beat up and the cold weather is getting harder for him to take. It sounded like he needs to find a new career soon. He must be doing something only a young man can handle."

"It's funny how little you know about your father. Mine comes home every night, but I don't know him much better. My parents are quite old, a lot older than the parents of other kids my age. Our schedules never cross and when I did play in a few ball games at school, my dad never came or showed any interest in what I was doing."

"At least we have each other." Josh said with a caring and longing smile. "Do you remember the lady I told you about that buys the five pairs of shoes every month? Well, she came in today and returned all five pair. She yelled at the manager, saying that he didn't know very much about shoes and she was going to take her business elsewhere."

"Oh brother," she rolled her eyes.

Josh continued, "How is the Professor doing on his case?"

"Now he's trying to find donut shops that will be the site of retribution. I'd like to help, but he won't let me. I think he's on the wrong track, anyway. I don't believe a crime has been committed just because somebody ate donuts in his car and had a note in the glove box with the partial name of a movie and a map to get to the theater."

"Maybe it was an outdoor theater and they ate the donuts for a snack." They both burst out in laughter, then Robin replied, "But you better not say that in front of the Professor."

They laughed again and then gave each other "the look," it was time to go. They gave each other their patented brief hug and Robin left for home.

Chapter 6

Days passed, most of them were routine. The puppies were moved into the main administration building and given a space in Professor Klueless's new office. Actually, Fred wanted to get them all out of his hair so he cleaned out an old storage area, put the Professor's desk in it, moved the puppies in and shut the door. The puppies had been left out as long as possible, but with no new home in sight; they needed to be brought in before winter. Actually, the Professor had been working hard on his case too, but he was getting nowhere. There were only a few weeks left before his deadline.

After the puppies were fed and exercised, Robin began to question the Professor about his progress. Robin knew that the computer was the best tool for the job, but since he was on the wrong trail, it really didn't matter.

Just as Robin was about to leave, the Professor started to get excited. He mumbled words to himself and then just got up and yelled to Robin, "Get the keys and let's go." Robin had no idea where, but was thrilled with the fact that she was actually being asked to be part of the team. In his haste, the Professor almost ran Fred over while Robin begged Fred for some keys, and yes, she got the tow truck again.

Robin popped into the driver's side and the Professor was already giving her instructions on how to get to their destination. The Professor had found a partial match to his cut outs. It was a donut shop on the lower side of town and its menu in the daily newspaper claimed they served items with a scrumptious mint frosting.

It took about twenty minutes before they pulled into the parking lot; this time it was a close squeeze for parking. The Professor asked Robin to stay in the truck in case it needed to be moved. The Professor bolted into the donut shop like a man with a mission. He looked at the two women standing behind the counter with their hands partially raised and said "I need some service here!" The women just moved their eyes away from the Professor and didn't move a muscle. The Professor said again a little louder, "I need some service over here, please." The clerks didn't even look at him this time. The Professor turned to the direction the clerks were looking and saw a man with his right hand in his jacket pocket and he had a shoulder holster partly revealed!

The Professor spoke again, this time at the man. "Now look here buddy, you undercover cops can't spend all your time monopolizing this place. There is real work that needs to be done." At that, the man took his hand out of his pocket and ran out the door! The Professor continued with the clerks, "Have you had any really dissatisfied customers with your mint-flavored donuts?" The clerks were silent for a minute and then relaxed a little and squeaked out a, "Not that we know of, sir."

With that, the Professor left in a huff about as fast as he had come in. As he got into the truck Robin asked him, "Any luck?"

"No, they haven't seen a thing. Let's drive around the block a few times before we head back. Maybe we can get a clue."

"Ok, there were two police cars that came into the lot while you were gone, but they couldn't find a place to park."

"I told you that this was a cop's hang out. No wonder they are never around when you need them."

They circled the block four times and the only thing that seemed out of place was the number of police cars parked around the block. Robin felt that it might be a high crime area, but the Professor insisted it was because of the donut shop and the lack of parking in the lot. In reality, the clerks at the donut shop had activated a silent alarm. A half dozen patrol cars had been dispatched, but the officers were trying to sneak up on the burglar. By the time they all arrived, only the clerks were in the shop.

The return trip for Robin and the Professor continued in a deafening silence. The Professor broke the silence and spoke in a broken voice, "Robin, I'm sorry if I've been a little rough with you, but many lives may be at stake if I don't solve this case. This maybe the most important case I have ever worked on."

Robin was stunned. This was the first time the Professor had ever come so close to an apology. "I'm sure I can help you if you only will let me," she responded.

"Lives are at stake, I just don't have the time to listen to all your ideas now. Maybe when this is all over we can have a long talk."

Robin thought to herself "I guess nothing has really changed" and returned to quietly driving back to "THE YARD."Then she thought, "I'll liven things up a bit.""Professor, do you know why there are so many pawn shops in old town?"

"Of course child, it's because they have so many more pieces on the board."

Robin thought about it for a second and then rolled her eyes and decided she would just drive.

Arriving at "THE YARD" both of them headed for the dog pen; the Professor's office. Although the puppies had been taken outside a few times a day, they had left behind wet newspapers and had chewed up everything in sight. Robin's backpack had been undisturbed on the Professor's desk except for one of the straps that had fallen within the pup-pies reach. Although they hadn't gotten it off the desk, it was wet and thoroughly chewed. She noticed the ring leader of the gang; it was the boy with the white stripe. "I've got a name for you, from

now on I'm going to call you Chewie."
The name fit. Robin wondered if Chewie
had been trying to get her backpack to
find additional food for the others.

Feeding time at the zoo had arrived,
so Robin got busy with her new respon-
sibilities. Professor Klueless sat down
and put his head in his hands; he knew
he needed a new approach. He hadn't
made enough progress on the case and
time was running out. He had added the
discovery of the mint ingredient and
possible match of the street location
to the original clues. He needed something more, but it wasn't coming to him
easily. Although he had been through
the car with a fine toothed comb, it was
the only place he could search for something new.

The Professor went back to the car
and began to search it all over again.
He noticed that the radio was tuned
to an AM radio station that was local
and broadcast in various languages
depending on the time of day, but never
in English. He had brought his small
portable vacuum and went over the truck
until every particle of dust from every
crevice was in the vacuum. Although he
had been over every inch of the car's
interior; he noticed stains on the gas
and brake pedal that he had previously

overlooked. He scraped off a small piece of the pedal with the unknown substance for further evaluation.

Back at his desk, Professor Klueless spread out his new evidence just as Robin was getting ready to leave. She stared at the new evidence that the Professor was so proud of and just shook her head in disbelief. Nothing looked remotely like a clue to her, but she wasn't the professional.

The puppies didn't want her to leave; they didn't get much attention during the day unless they did something wrong. They were all over her legs until she lost her balance and landed on the floor, to the puppies delight. She squealed a little, happy for the moment until one of the puppies licked her on the lips. That ended that whole play secession and she left in a hurry, rubbing her sleeve over her mouth in disgust.

Professor Klueless didn't even look up as she left, concentrating on what tests to run on his new evidence. After Robin had gone, Professor Klueless studied his clues. The first one he selected to investigate was the substance from the car's foot pedals. He took the sample and inserted it into the spectrophotometer. Behold, a prism of light which corresponded to the unique properties of oil. The only problem was that he had forgotten how to interpret the results. Even then he had lost the standard so the results had little value. Then it hit him. Dutch could do it. The idea was so simple; he would pour ten samples of oil, each in a separate cup and let Dutch sniff the sample and tell him which cup it matched.

From the supply area, he selected ten Ball canning jars and went to find the oils for the test. He used peanut oil, motor oil, canola oil, tanning oil, vegetable oil, palm oil, etc.; all put in a row about three feet apart in front of a decorative wooden fence. Then he went to the door and called Dutch. Dutch hadn't been used for this kind of work in a long time. He came prancing to Klueless on the first call. Klueless held out the sample and spoke to Dutch almost in a whisper, "Ok boy, go find the cup with the same oil in it as this," as he held out the sample from the pedals. Dutch looked a little confused at this request, but started toward the oil jars. Klueless was really disappointed as Dutch sniffed all ten jars. Ok, one down, time to try number two.

"Here boy, go find the cup with the same smell." Dutch was beginning to catch on to the game and since he had sampled the smell of each, he went right to the jar with the palm oil in it, sat down and barked. The Professor knew he had found the answer to his question. He made Dutch go through the test a few more times but he consistently led to the palm oil. Klueless was on cloud nine and gave Dutch a big squeeze. The Professor knew that palm oil was the preferred oil for making donuts. You could almost hear Dutch say, "You're welcome," as he went back on patrol. Now the Professor had no doubt that he was on the right track. It seemed kind of ironic that his case was leading to a donut shop. The Professor had always felt guilty about spending so much time in donut shops when he should have spent more time on his cases. Although, he still solved more than his share. He always wonder how many more cased he could have solved if he didn't have the addiction for fresh donuts.

The next challenge was to analyze the contents of the vacuum. Klueless opened it up and poured out the dust onto a clean white rag. By observation, there was nothing recognizable by shape or color. The Professor bent down to see if it had any distinguishable odor. Boom! The door opened so hard it slammed against the wall. Klueless hit the dust and it scattered into the air, gone forever. Fred had entered with a bang and was not a happy camper. "Professor," he shouted with a look that could kill. "When are you going to get your dogs out of my building?" The Professor was in shock that Fred had called the dogs his, but also upset that his final clue was now gone forever.

"Why did you call them my dogs?" fired back the Professor,

"Well, they're not mine and they're in your office. Don't you think they are your responsibility to get rid of? I didn't find them, or feed them or give them shelter." Then Fred turned around and left in a huff, just as fast as he came in.

The Professor was thinking to himself, "What was that all about? Well, I have gotten all the clues that I'm going to get. Let's see :"

1. Someone is going to get even by the end of the month for bad mint.
2. The map indicated a pattern of streets on the lower side of town.
3. The man or group that is going to commit this crime may not have English as their first language.

4. The individual involved in this potential crime has been around and stepping in palm oil.

"Every clue seems to indicate that the crime had to be attempted in or near the donut shop, and soon. Maybe I should monitor the police radio and see if other crimes can be connected to this one," he mused. The Professor went into the salvage room again and came back to his office with a police scanner. He turned it on and it lit up, but the sound was distorted. Nothing was going on now, but he decided to listen to it for the next few days.

Chapter 7

While all these things were taking place back at "THE YARD"; Robin was arriving at her favorite shoe store. She was late and Josh was worried that she wouldn't come at all. He had already left the observation window and was cleaning and restocking the shelves. As Robin came in, he heard the door and yelled, "Sorry we're closed. Please come back tomorrow. We open at 9:30."

Robin playing along, said, "I can't come back at 9:30; I'll be in school."

Robin and Josh were alone in the store. Grandpa had left for the day and Josh was to lock up when he was finished. He went and locked the door so no customers would come in and then came over to Robin for a hug, their usual greeting. Both of them sat down in the customer's area to catch up on their daily activities.

Josh gestured to Robin to go first, so she cleared her throat, took a deep breath and started, "The Professor and I drove to a donut shop about twenty minutes away in old town and questioned the clerks about either bad mint as an ingredient, or a bad batch of donuts. We didn't get any good information at all, but we did see a lot of cop cars in the area. I had to drive the old tow truck. This time it was harder to park so I had to wait in the truck until the Professor was done. He wasn't gone long, but I wish he would have brought me back a chocolate donut."

"What's old town like now? I haven't been there in years."

"It hasn't changed a lot; I mean, the buildings are all the same." She waited a second for a response and then continued, "Just getting more and more run down. There is a lot more litter and people sprawling in the walkways. It kind of gives you the creeps just being there."

"I guess I haven't missed much by not being there."

"It's strange there now. Many of the buildings are unoccupied, and the businesses that have stayed are a lot different. Like, there is a large tattoo parlor, pawn shops and small grocery stores. It's funny though, the old bank building looked unoccupied, but there was a lot of smoke coming from a new smoke stack. It just looked out of place."

"Maybe they put in a new wood stove in the middle of the floor to dance around all night."

"Funny man! What happened around here?"

"We had a few customers this morning, lunch time was busy, not much going on this afternoon. Grandfather, left early and asked me to lockup."

"I'm glad you waited for me." Their hands inadvertently touched; both of them were aware of it and a little spark went through them.

"Have you ever wondered what things will be like ten years from now? Look how much old town has changed," Josh stated.

"I hope I'm married and live in small, clean town miles away from here with pretty houses and a big grassy yard with lot of green trees. Where do you want to be?"

"Well, not in this shoe store. I hope to be done with college and working in a job where I can build things." This was not the response Robin was fishing for.

"It's hard to think about the future when we don't understand the present or even the past."

"The past, why worry about the past?" She asked a little disappointed that the discussion was going the wrong way.

"Did you ever wonder where we came from or even why we're here? I know what we have been told, but who knows what really happened thousands of years ago. What about this whole Bible thing that keeps on coming up, where people are dying rather than giving up their beliefs. They weren't here thousands of years ago, so why die over it?"

"Does it really matter what happened in the past, isn't it more important to think about the future?"

"Sure the future is important, but what if we're alive for some purpose and we miss it? There has to be more of a purpose for life than just working in a shoe store."

Josh was Robin's first, and maybe only love, and she was hoping he felt the same way she did. She was aware of how special he was and hoped to get confirmation that he felt the same way about her. At times it seemed he felt it too, but then just as the fire was starting to burn, it would go out as quickly as it started.

"Do you really believe we evolved from monkeys and then back to some original big bang?"

"Josh, we're alone in this dimly lit store and all you want to talk about is monkeys?" Robin was ticked off. She got up from the chair and bolted out the door with no hug. Normally, she was so timid and afraid to show anger, but this time she got mad and left in a huff. She questioned herself while she walked at a runners pace. (What horrible thing did Josh really do to get her so angry?) She was really angry though.

When Robin got home, her parent questioned her a little about being late but seemed to accept the fact that she had to drive the Professor to old town. They didn't know the people at "THE YARD", but hadn't heard anything bad about them either. Beside, that's where the police station was located so it couldn't be too bad.

After Robin ate the supper her mom reheated, she did her homework and went to bed. As she lay there staring at the ceiling, she was sorry she had gotten angry with Josh, her only true friend. Not only did it not make any sense even to her; what if Josh was right? Maybe we are here on earth for a purpose greater than a daily routine. She had never thought about such a question before. She had taken whatever her teacher had told her over the years as fact, it had never really mattered much to daily living anyway. What mattered most to her was if Josh cared for her as much as she cared for him. She couldn't bear to think of a life without him. Tomorrow, she would apologize to him and hope she hadn't damaged their friendship.

Chapter 8

The Professor had been over his clues hundreds of times. There was only one solution and the retribution had to take place at that donut shop. All the evidence pointed that way and there was no way to get additional evidence. Just then, he heard the scanner break the squelch, "All cars code 7 in Old Town, all cars proceed with caution to Arnold's Gun Sales & Repair." It was repeated several more times, and he knew a code 7 was an armed robbery in progress, "proceed quietly and with caution." He had been listening to the scanner for a few days and heard about traffic stops, domestic disturbances, and even petty theft, but this was the first happening in Old Town that could have significance to his case. He then turned on his AM radio to the frequency of "always news" and listened for the developments. The announcer reported the call of police action in Old Town and that further reports would be given when made available. He turned up the volume on both radios and listened intently.

Bang! Fred slammed the door open again, "What's all the noise coming from here?"

"Would you please be quiet?" pleaded the Professor.

"Now look, there is enough noise in here with those crazy dogs barking all the time, we don't need radios blaring. As soon as those dogs are old enough, I want them gone."

"I don't like the dogs in here either, but right now I need to hear these radio reports. It's a matter of life and death."

This business has been a dedicated service for over forty-five years, but we never had problems like this, Fred hollered. He stormed out and Robin walked in. Robin asked, "What did they name that storm that just left?"

"Quiet, I need to hear the radios."

"What's going on?"

"I'll tell you later, quiet p-l-e-a-s-e."

Strange as it seemed to him, every day began after school hours about the time that Robin would arrive. She began to feed the puppies in silence. Then her ear caught the AM radio, "An armed robbery has just taken place in Old Town at Arnold's Gun Shop. Four men, all just less than 6 feet tall, slender, looking to be in their late twenties, made a clean get-away before police arrived. Arnold, the owner, reported to authorities that about ten military type rifles and four 45 caliber hand guns were stolen. The robbers filled their pockets with ammunition as they fled on foot. The police have no clues at this time."

The Professor turned off the AM radio and told Robin to stop feeding the puppies and get the keys from Fred. Fred was all too happy to let them go, but not all the dogs got their supper. Either way, he would not get the peace and quiet he craved.

The Professor and Robin fled to the truck like Batman and his side kick Robin, scurrying to the scene of the crime with no lack of concern for any danger along the way. It was just before rush hour and driving the old truck had at least one redeeming quality; every driver gave them the right-of-way.

Once they arrived in Old Town, the traffic was normal and there was no trace of the crime. The number of police cars seemed normal; the Professor thought that there were too few for a major donut area. They were driving around the block, looking for clues, when they heard a siren behind them. As they pulled to the curb they heard the police over the loud speaker; "Get out of the car and place your hands on the roof." Robin was quick to respond, but the Professor was insulted. She began to plead with him to comply rather than make this a real disaster. He finally got out of the truck, but refused to comply. He stared at the officer right in the face and dared him to back up his command. Fortunately, the officer noticed his age and lack of a threat and walked over with his gun out, but not pointed directly at the Professor.

The officer spoke, "What's your business here and let's see some ID's." The second officer took Robin's drivers license and the Professor's AARP card over to the car and called them in. "We observed you going around the block several times and we need to know your business here."

Before the Professor responded, the second police officer motioned to the arresting office that it was ok. "Don't worry about the Professor; he's from "THE YARD."

The first officer returned his gun to its holster and seemed to become friendlier, but the Professor was angry that he had been challenged. "You had no cause to stop us. We didn't commit any crime" barked the Professor. Robin just covered her eyes with her hands and began to pray the Professor would back down.

"Sorry Sir, we didn't know who you were and there was a hold-up here a few hours ago. We're just being cautious. Besides, there are no license plates on the truck."

"If you wouldn't spend all your time around donut shops, you could be finding the real criminals."

The first officer stated again, "I'm sorry sir, but we didn't know who you were." He then returned to his car and drove off quickly.

"Why did you let that old man get away with talking to you that way?", the junior officer asked his partner.

The first officer, senior by twenty years, replied, "Son, that's one guy you don't want to mess with."

"He's a crabby old man, what's he got on you?"

"Years ago I tried to arrest that man for speeding. He seemed old twenty years ago, but speaking to him was like talking

to a porcupine. He never quite understood, and never quit jabbing. After a
few hours and the worst migraine I ever
had; I released him for the good of the
department. Besides later I found out
he was with the detective unit."

Robin and the Professor were returning
to "THE YARD" but the reason for the
police action was killing her. "Why
did that officer let you go so easily?"
she asked.

"Didn't you hear him Robin? He didn't
know who I was."

It was quiet in the truck all the way
back to "THE YARD." When they went in
to the Professor's office, they noticed
that two of the pups were missing. Robin
dashed to find Fred and get the 411.

"I told you that the dogs had to go
as soon as possible," Fred said with
a stern expression on his face. "It
just so happened that I found a home
for two pups. You had to feed them by
hand anyway; the new owner could do it
the same as you." Robin quickly scanned
over the puppies to see if Chewie and
Princess were still there. They were and
that gave her some consolation.

Robin didn't reply for some time. She
was stunned that it happened so unex-
pectedly. "Do you think that they will
make it alright?"

"They'll make it ok. Look at it this way, you did the best you could and now you have help. We'll find homes for the others soon. After all, Dutch has a good reputation and is respected by many of the people in this area. It won't take long to find good homes now that people know we have them and that they are ready for a new home."

All Robin could think of was that it happened so fast, and she didn't even get to say goodbye to the pups. Her whole attitude toward them changed now that she realized they could be gone at any time. It didn't seem quite as much of a chore to feed them; she needed to pack her love for them into the little time that was left.

Just then, there was a loud bark at the door. Fred got up and went over to see what the problem was. Dutch was the only dog allowed in "THE YARD", but he never came into the admin building. He opened the door and Dutch walked right by him and into the Professor's office. Dutch looked over the puppies until his eyes rested on Chewie. Then without a sound, he went over to him, grabbed him by the scruff of the neck and proudly walked through the open doors and into "THE YARD." Evidently, he had chosen his replacement, someone he could personally train to become the "keeper of "THE YARD." Fred turned to Robin and said, "If royalty chose Chewie as his replacement, you had better find another name for him."

"I guess," said Robin with a deep sigh. "There are not many puppies left either."

It was getting so late by the time Robin got to the shoe store that it was closed and dark inside. The unthinkable had happened. Josh had left and Robin had to live another day with the concern that she would not be forgiven. That was a huge weight for a young girl to carry, especially since she only had one true love and may never have another.

Going to bed was easy. Going to sleep seemed impossible. Robin just laid there with too much on her mind. Things were happening much too fast. In the last few weeks she found the puppies, now they were already going away, the Professor was now showing her some attention, but with it came responsibility as she realized she needed to protect him. Just as her relationship with Josh was turning into real love, she had thoughts that she might be losing him for good. As the night continued, exhaustion won and she fell asleep.

Chapter 9

The next day, while Robin was in school; she was called to the office to see the principal. She was unaware that she had done anything wrong, her grades were good, although they had slipped in the last few weeks. The office seemed a long way to go with all these thoughts going through her mind, but the request seemed to have some urgency attached to it.

Robin knocked on the principal's door and heard the voice inside say to come in and sit down. The principal was on the phone, trying to locate one of Robin's parents for some kind of permission. She put down the phone and with no greeting began to speak in a very serious tone. "I just received a call from "THE YARD."Seems a very important Professor by the name of Klueless has requested that you come to "THE YARD" as soon as possible. I've been trying to get in contact with your parents for permission, but have not been able to reach them. But, since it was "THE YARD" who requests your presence; I'm not sure I can prevent it. Why they need to see you so desperately is beyond me, but you had better comply. Do you know where it is, child?"

"Yes ma'am, I do. I'll go over there immediately." Robin thought if they only knew the Professor, they would have never given permission. The Professor had never had a real emergency in his life.

As soon as she left the principal's office, she double timed the jaunt to "THE YARD."Arriving out of breath and through gasps of air asked Fred where the Professor was. Fred pointed to his office with a look on his face that said, "Where else would he be?" As she went in, the Professor was frantic; "Boy, am I glad to see you! I just heard on the police radio that there was an increase in traffic near the Old Town tattoo parlor. It seems that the joint has been buzzing with traffic all morning. There is something going on, maybe it has to do with the donut shop being nearby."

Robin and the Professor ran past Fred, who just threw Robin the keys and they were on their way. They left so fast,

Robin didn't even notice that another puppy was missing.

The drive to Old Town was becoming routine. Robin easily found a parking place right in front of the tattoo parlor. As usual, the Professor went busting right in; unaware that the police had a silent stakeout on the place. The Professor got into a heated discussion with the first tattoo artist he found. By the time Robin caught up, they were in the middle of an argument about guns and mints. Both were getting extremely out of hand, so she tugged at the Professor until she pulled him out the door. With the activity building, Robin felt it was a good idea to get the Professor out of there, post haste.

That was all the police needed, they came rushing into the place with under-cover agents, completely unaware to the Professor. The police rushed the place with a half dozen officers from all doors. Then they brought a dog unit, prepared for anything. Once the dog unit was in the place, they barked and growled uncontrollably. The police went to a back closet where large supplies of drugs were found.

Robin and the Professor were already on their way back to "THE YARD." After entering the office, they turned on the police scanner and then the AM radio to the news station. It seems that about the same time they were in Old Town, the police had uncovered the biggest drug bust in the history of the area. Robin and the Professor just looked at each other as if to say, "I wonder why we didn't see any police activity going on?"

It was too late for Robin to return to school, so she decided to feed the puppies and make sure that she got to the shoe store before closing. As she rounded up the dogs, she became aware that another dog was missing. At this rate, they would all be gone in no time.

The Professor was sure that he was on the right track with the donut shop being the target and that the tattoo parlor workers somehow would figure in. Their shop was close to the donut shop, so they had opportunity to get bad donuts. If they did get bad donuts, then they would have motive.

Robin was a hugger, so she gave each puppy a hug and rushed out the door to see Josh. Fred and the Professor didn't even acknowledge her as she left, which was more usual than not. Actually, Robin was beginning to understand the Professor's ways and even feel sorry for him. Neither of them had many friends and in the Professor's case, all he had to be proud of was his past. She had not known him in his prime and didn't know if he had always been absentminded, but he couldn't help who he had become in his old age.

Robin headed to her next stop. She was early today but Josh was not at the window. It could be because she was early; she hoped it wasn't because he was mad. Robin entered the store and Josh was waiting on a lady customer. She could tell that it was difficult for him and could see that he had a desire to be more than a shoe salesman. He had never talked about any real passions in his life and not much of his past either. Although she loved him dearly, she didn't know much about him or his family. She just knew that he was the only one for her and he made her feel like nothing else in life mattered.

Robin waited until the last customer left and then approached Josh. "Are you angry with me? I'm so sorry that I ran out of here the other day after being quite rude."

"No. I'm not mad, but I don't understand either."

"Josh, I care for you so much but I'm afraid that you don't care for me in the same way."

"Robin, you're the best friend I ever had."

"Josh, I want you to be more than just a best friend."

Josh became quiet as if he was trying to process exactly what she meant by her remark. Then he spoke tenderly, "Robin, I care for you more than I have cared for anyone else in my life, but this is new ground for me too."

Robin smiled. She would be happy with that, at least for now. "Promise we can always be best friends?"

Just then, Grandpa, the owner of the store came in and started to give Josh a lecture. "This is a place of business; you can do your socializing after hours. I'm not paying you to gab all day." With that, Josh went back to work and Robin wished she had not come early. At least then they would have been alone for a few minutes after hours. She looked at her watch to see the time and decide if she should wait until closing or just come back tomorrow at the usual time. She decided that it would be better for Josh if she came back, so she started home. She had to keep reminding herself that Josh had said he cared for her more than he had cared for anyone, that would have to be enough for now.

Robin arrived home early, and was actually on time for supper. She sat at the table and tried to talk to her mother about her dilemma, something she hadn't done in years. Her mom was busy preparing the meal but noticed that her little girl was growing up and seemed to have a lot on her mind. "Do you want to talk about it Honey?"

"Talk about what?"

"Whatever it is that you're in such deep thought about?"

"I don't think you would understand, Mom." Replied Robin.

"I was young once too, Honey. Why don't you give me a try?"

This was something new for Robin. She had internalized her feelings for years and not let anyone but Josh into her private world.

"It's just a boy, Mom, you won't understand. I don't understand myself. When I'm around him nothing else matters. When I'm not around him; he's all I think about."

"It sounds serious. It's about your age that love comes knocking for the first time."

"I think I do love him Mom, but I'm afraid he doesn't love me. To him we're just good friends."

"That's a good start, Honey. If it's meant to be, it will grow. If it doesn't; God will bring into your life the right person. Just watch for God's guidance and don't get ahead of him and make a mistake. Living with the right man can be the most wonderful gift in life. Living with the wrong man can be one of the biggest mistakes you'll ever make."

"You're starting to talk like Josh; what does God have to do with it?"

"God is more than just the creator of the world. He cares about people in a personal way and actually is with them all through life. Don't you remember what you were taught in church? If you put your trust in Him, He will never leave you and He can be closer than a brother."

"Thanks Mom, but right now I'll settle for Josh to be closer than a brother." With that, Robin got up and went to her room. "Call me when supper's ready," she yelled as she was half way up the stairs. Her mother's words would come to her mind again as she laid in bed that night.

"God, if what Mom said is true; I want you to be my best friend. Please, make Josh my special friend too." Then she drifted off to sleep, more peacefully than usual.

Chapter 10

It was almost midnight, when the phone rang, waking Robin's mother from a sound sleep. She tried to wake up her husband, but he only rolled over and snored louder. She had a decision to make. It seems a Professor from "THE YARD" was on the phone and needed Robin immediately. Her mother didn't understand at all what was going on, but was afraid not to comply with an important man from "THE YARD." It was too late for Robin to go alone, so she would have to get dressed and drive her over to "THE YARD." She hurried to Robin's room to awaken her first, before she threw on her clothes.

Robin didn't want her mother finding out what was going on. She knew that would end the few friendships she was trying so hard to develop. Actually, her Mom wouldn't even think "THE YARD" was a proper place for a young girl. She needed to think fast. She put a pair of slacks over her pajamas and a light coat and ran for the family car. "It's ok Mom. This is something I have to do myself." Robin's mom ran to the phone and hit redial, but no one answered. Her next step was to call the police department, she had no way to getting to "THE YARD", they only had one car. She dialed 911.

"Emergency and Name?" the operator asked.

Robin's mother was unsure. She didn't have time for this and couldn't decide if this would constitute a real emergency either. She hung up, got to her knees and prayed, "Lord, I don't know what's going on, but protect Robin whatever she is involved in."

Robin made it to "THE YARD" in record time. Driving sure was faster than walking home every night. "THE YARD" was locked for the night so she got out of the car and used the call box.

"Professor, this is Robin, you called?"

"I'll open the gate and you can drive up. We need to get to Old Town."

"Professor, its midnight and my parents are going to be really mad, this better be really important."

"Just drive up and I'll get the truck keys and meet you."

Robin was thinking, *"Oh goodie, I get to drive big bertha to Old Town at night. What a great way to spend an evening. I'd rather be home in bed. I wonder what the big deal is. Probably the Professor heard on the police radio someone got busted for "Jay walking."*

"Robin, I'm so glad you're here. As I was shutting off the radios to go home, I heard that an armed man was captured by two police at the Old Town Donut Shop."

"Let me check it out. Is there a computer in the office?"

"I think there is one on Fred's desk."

"Boy, this is so archaic. It is on the internet, though. Just let me get to the local news website for channel four."

"What's that? We really don't have time for this. We need to go now!"

"Just a second, I've got it. It says here that two cops were in the back waiting for the donuts to come out of the oven. A man entered, showed a gun, and asked for the money in the cash register. There wasn't any money; it had been taken to the bank at the end of the sales day. They were only open for baking. Evidently, he got so angry that he got louder and louder in his demand. The two police officers in the kitchen heard him and snuck up behind him."

"See, don't you understand, the redemption is about to begin."

"Why do you think that? It sounds like it was just a simple burglary?"

"No, no, the man must have been one of the guys who stole all those guns from Arnold's Gun Shop. He just got tired and hungry waiting for the retribution to begin. He probably has a whole group of help just waiting for him to return with the donuts. We don't have any time to argue now, let's get going."

"My parents are going to be so mad, but let's go."

Professor Klueless threw her the keys to their favorite truck and both of them ran for it. The whole way to Old Town the Professor was trying to get Robin to go faster and faster. She remembered the last time they were stopped by the police, and she didn't want to try to explain any more to her parents more than she had to. They did make it in record time, but Robin was scared the whole time expecting to hear sirens.

They pulled into the bakery parking lot and tried to look in through the front window for any action. They could see a light in the back, but no one was in the customer area. Robin couldn't understand why they were there anyway; the crime had taken place over an hour and a half ago. Finally, Robin volunteered to go up to the front door and knock. It seemed to her it was better to speed things up rather than just sit in the parking lot. Robin jumped out of the truck and started to the front door. When the Professor saw what she was doing, he got all excited. "No! Don't go - we need to watch for more gunmen to come and see what happened to the other guy."

As she headed for the door of the truck, the Professor slid over into the driver's seat and started the truck while motioning Robin to come back. While she was walking back to the truck, which was on the far side of the lot, the Professor thought they could save time if he met her half way. He pulled the gear shift down towards drive, but it went too far and engaged into reverse. The Professor panicked and tried to slam on the brake, but his foot slid off and hit the gas. The truck flew right by Robin in reverse and headed for the old bank building across the street. The truck hit the front door of the bank with a tremendous force! In seconds, there was a hole in the front of the old bank big enough to fly a plane through.

The truck engine died after the collision, leaving the Professor behind the wheel in an utter panic. Robin ran over to see if the Professor was injured. As she did, four police cars pulled up with sirens and lights flashing. The police ran up to the truck with guns drawn. Robin grimaced. Nothing would ever make this right with her parents. She would be grounded until the end of time. The police saw the Professor behind the wheel with his hands over his eyes. Just as the tension began to relax, one police noticed a lot of movement and noise coming from the bank's vault area. Their attention was transferred to the vault and the Professor became a secondary issue.

One of the first policemen who arrived yelled, "Halt! You're covered."

A barrage of bullets hit the air.

"Shots fired, send more back up to the old town bank building."

Robin heard the shots, jumped into the truck and hit the floor, pulling the Professor with her. Additional police cars filled the alley in the back of the building. The police didn't return fire, but set up their positions. A swat team was requested, which was the only noise filling the complete silence. Now it was a waiting game; the suspects surrounded.

"We have you surrounded, throw out your weapons and come out with your hands up," was shouted over the police car's loud speaker. Everything was quiet - too quiet.

The Professor stuck his head out the truck widow and spoke to the officer nearest him; "Don't worry, you can wait them out. The thief from the bakery never got back with the donuts. They will starve without food." The officer had to breakout with a small grin in spite of the tense situation. The sharp-shooters were in place, and the sudden stillness was deafening. The Professor turned on the truck radio full blast to the local news station. His intent was to find the station he found the radio tuned to in "THE YARD."He couldn't remember what the frequency was though. The men in the bank vault heard the radio announcer say; "Police have a gang of crooks pinned down in Old Town. Sharp-shooters are in place, it looks like this will get bloody before it's over. Keep tuned for minute to minute updates from Old Town."

The gang members looked at each other; they hadn't realized how hope-less their situation was. One by one, they threw out their handguns and the leader, in broken English yelled, "Don't shoot! We're coming out. Don't shoot!" A total of seven men came out of the bank vault with their hands in the air. The police rushed in and escorted the men into the back of four police cars. As the policemen re-entered the bank, they saw a huge furnace being used to melt down jewelry from previous thefts. No wonder one of the gang members referred to this old bank building as "the mint." It was the biggest fencing operation the police had ever uncovered.

The sun was coming up as Robin arrived home in the back of a police car. Her parents came rushing out of the house, crying. They didn't know the details, but were glad to see Robin alive and apparently in fairly good shape. She was tired though, and after a few hugs requested that she be allowed to go to bed and wait to talk about the situation later. Her parents agreed, thanked the police for bringing her home and went into the house. They sat at the breakfast table and brought out the coffee as they tried to prepare themselves for the story they would hear in a couple of hours. At least Robin was ok and the police said that she wasn't in any trouble. That gave them enough consolation to be able to wait.

When Robin awoke, she went to her parents and pieced the story together the best she could. It was almost noon, so school today was not an option. Her biggest desire was to get to Josh and share this experience with him. Her parents gave her permission to go see Josh, but she had to come right back home afterward.

Robin got cleaned up and started out for the shoe store. It was the middle of the afternoon and she was hoping that she and Josh could get a few minutes alone together. She entered the store with her mind still trying to find a way to tell Josh about the whole experience. She looked around, but Josh's grandfather was the only one in the store.

"Where is Josh?"

"I'm sorry Robin, he's not here. He has gone to be with his father."

"With his father, when will he be back?" Terror gripped her - this was worse than the feelings she had at the bank.

"He didn't say. He received a phone call from his father, had me call the airline for a flight, packed a suitcase, and left for Canada to meet him. I assume his father gave him specific instructions on the phone; Josh has been wanting to talk to his father for some time. I'm not sure when to expect him back. Would you like to work here until he does?"

Robin began to sob, ran out of the store and straight home to her room. Her parents were still talking at the table and wondered what could have happened now. What could have been worse than what Robin had already been through?

Chapter 11

Josh had a seat on a small aircraft bound for another country; something he had never done before. Actually, this was his first flight, at least the first one he remembered. He tried to concentrate on what he was going to say to his father and was curious that his dad suddenly wanted to see him in person. He tried to remember his mother, but that didn't work. She had been out of his life for so long; all he could remember were bits and pieces that others had told him. Now he was on his way to see his father, a man he barely knew. He had seen his dad every year for a couple of months, but never even had a real conversation with him.

His dad was always tired and kept to himself except for a few late night talks with Grandfather. Why his dad had not been a part of his life, he didn't know and rarely cared. Things had a way of going from day to day with enough daily problems to keep him from asking the deep questions. That is until now. Now he wanted to know who he was and where he was going in life. He could have waited until summer when his dad came for R&R, but this time his dad called him with some urgency. Actually, he didn't even completely know where he was going. A car was to pick him up at the airport and take him to his dad. If he were more imaginative, he could have built up the notion that he was going to be held for ransom.

The flight was short, less than two hours. With takeoff and landing times, it was only an hour to quietly have his mind go crazy. After landing, he disembarked and walked into the terminal. It didn't seem at all like this in the movies. He saw a large line for international passengers and decided that was the place to go; at the end of the line. The customs and security screening was not eventful, just slow. He hadn't realized it, but his mind was working overtime as he began to contemplate what he was actually doing. His mind flashed back to Robin and he realized he had left so quickly, he hadn't had a chance to tell her what he was doing. Besides, he couldn't call her from here either; he had to leave his cell phone behind. It actually belonged to Grandpa and was on the store's service plan.

Once outside the airport, he looked for his ride. Next to a large black limo was a uniformed man with a sign with his name on it. He wondered how much money his dad spent on the limo, it was huge for just one guy. The driver confirmed Josh's identity and held the door for him to enter the large back seat. Once in, Josh felt he could get lost in this thing. No matter how hard he tried to get comfortable, he couldn't. He was definitely out of his comfort zone.

"Where are we going?" asked Josh with more than a little apprehension

"The stadium Sir. Feel free to take a drink and some of the munchies."

It was about a fifteen minute ride to the stadium. It looked large, like everything else this morning. It was strange to see such a big place with hardly anyone around it.

The driver stopped, came and opened the back door for Josh, and pointed toward the administration building. "Your father is in the office, Son. He is waiting for you."

Josh hadn't felt fear on the trip before now, but he didn't know what to expect either. Inside the office it looked like any other office with a few busy people and at least one computer on every desk. He noticed his dad motioning him into a private office in the corner of the large room. It was like being summed into the principal's office for the first time.

"I'm glad you could make it, Son, and you came so fast. I'm impressed."

"On the phone, you sounded urgent."

"Well, yes and no. We have needed this talk for a long time and I wanted to do this face to face. Your grandfather felt it couldn't wait until after the season."

"Season?"

"I'm sorry I have neglected you for all these years. I was a professional football player, and when your mother died I just didn't know how to relate to a young child. As the years passed, my body didn't hold up really well and I wasn't the easiest person to be around. Grandpa has done such a good job of taking care of you that it was easier to just let things go by from year to year. I had to be on the road a lot anyway, even when I switched to coaching. I'm sorry I've neglected you for so many years. I never did get over losing your mother."

"I'm sorry too Dad. Do we have a future together?"

"Son, my days are getting shorter. You're just beginning your life. I have accepted a coaching job in the NFL so I will be in the country at least. I expect that you have some idea of what you what to do with your life. Do you want to get into the shoe store business with Grandpa?"

"Dad, that's not what I have in mind. I hope to attend college for at least four years. I want to build things that I can be proud of, things with lasting value."

"Like what?"

"That's what I'm not sure of, but I have always been interested in science, maybe in physics or bio-chemistry."

"Well, we don't have to know that just yet, the important part is if we want to go down this road together."

"Yes Dad, together." They both smiled and for the first time; they began a real relationship.

"Well, why don't you come and live with me and start college there. You don't even have to declare a major for the first year or two."

"Two problems, Dad; where are you going? Then there is Robin."

"Robin?"

"Dad, she has been the only person in my whole life that I could just talk to. Just to be around her makes me feel like everything is worthwhile. I can't just leave her; I think I love her." After Josh said it, he realized for the first time that he did love her.

"Love! You're so young. However, I remember my young days and the way your mother made me feel. Let me call your grandfather to tell him to find a new clerk and fill him in on the new job. Then we can talk more about school and Robin."

"So where are we going, Dad?"

"Well," he said with a smile, "I've had enough cold days, our new home is in Arizona.

"Arizona? Never been there, is it hot?"

"Boy is it ever!"

Josh's dad put his big arm around him and they headed out together toward the cafeteria to continue the discussion. To Josh, it was a dream come true. His father wasn't leaving him, his father loved him.

Chapter 12

Robin started another day with the old routine; school, Dutch, "THE YARD", but no Josh. The part of the day that mattered most was gone. In school, Robin had become quite popular, at least for a few days. Since Robin and the Professor made headlines as being instrumental in the capture of a gang of thieves; everybody wanted a piece of her. With all the attention focused on her, she wished she could have back the old days; they were boring, but peaceful. After school, as per her unwritten schedule, she found her beloved Dutch and Chewie. Yes, that name had to be changed. For now, though, all she could think of was "Dutch II." It wouldn't work though; "Here Dutch the second," sounded odd. No, not happening. After Dutch worked with the pup for a while; a name would develop with along with his character.

Her thoughts changed to Fred and the Professor. She passed through the gate and into the admin building; everything seemed the same. Robin scanned the offices and only saw one dog left. She turned to Fred, who anticipated the question. "That's right Robin, only one pup left. With all the publicity, it didn't take long for the pups to get new homes. Only Princess is left, if you want her." Robin began to cry. It would be unbearable if she lost Princess too. "Of course I want her, can you keep her another day to two until I clear it with my parents?"

"Sure, having one in the building is better than having seven."

"Maybe to you, but they all loved me and I felt needed."

"The Professor needs you too, better go in and see him. He's been quite busy the last few weeks, but now he needs a reason to go on again."

Robin went through door number two and saw the Professor just sitting at his desk, his head in his hands. There were no maps, no open phone books and no enthusiasm on his face. The Professor saw Robin enter and in a soft voice said, "It was fun while it lasted, wasn't it?"

"I've been worried about you the last few weeks. You drove yourself so hard, didn't get much food or sleep, but you did have purpose."

"Everyone needs a purpose. Thanks for helping me; I couldn't have done it without you."

"Wow, that was one of the nicest things anybody has ever said to me. By the way, do you think I should take Princess home with me before I get permission? I mean, do you think it would help having Mom look into those cute little eyes?"

"Yours or the dogs?" They both laughed; actually, for the first time.

The next day started the routine all over again. The morning promised the beginning of a beautiful day. The sun was just about to break through the clouds. Dutch and Chewie were on patrol following the stone wall, seeking anything suspicious. Suddenly Chewie, who was following Dutch, dashed in front of him and tried to keep him from going further. Dutch took this as a warning and stopped, listened intently, and smelled in every direction. He couldn't sense any problem, so he pushed Chewie aside and continued his patrol. Chewie bit at Dutch's tail, but he just turned around and gave Chewie "the look.

There was no other option, Chewie ran at Dutch full speed, barking and growling. Without warning, a large cougar jumped after him. Chewie tried to find small clearances the cat couldn't get through to hide in, but the cat was fast and smart. Now Dutch understood. Chewie had been trying to save him. His senses had eroded over the years, but not his spirit. It took a few seconds before he caught up to the cat, but when he did; he didn't hold anything back. The snarling, biting and clawing continued for what seemed like an eternity to Chewie. When the dust settled, the wounded cat dragged itself away and Dutch just lay there, bleeding profusely. Chewie ran over to Dutch to see if he could help, but he couldn't even move him to a hiding place. He had to get help fast. Chewie ran toward the admin building as fast as he could go. "Over the river and through the woods" had a whole new meaning now. Once he reached the outside door to the building, he barked, screeched, and howled.

Fred, who was always near the front yelled to the Professor, "What is wrong with your dog?"

"He's not my dog, but I never heard a dog make such a fuss. You'd better find out what he wants."

Fred opened the door slowly to peek out first, but Chewie was through the door and upon him. He could not be quieted.

"Better see if he wants you to follow him" yelled the Professor.

"Ok Chewie, show me, show me boy."

Chewie took off like there was no tomorrow. Fred started to run after him and yelled to the Professor, "Get a couple of the officers and follow me. Looks like we're going into the wooded section of 'THE YARD'" he said. Fred continued to follow but the distance between him and Chewie grew larger. Chewie became aware of that and doubled back as to not lose him. Chewie stopped and looked over a furry bunch of leaves. Fred saw Dutch. He was gripped with pure emotion. Tears came to his eyes as he approached and bent down to stroke Dutch. "It will be ok, boy." This was the biggest lie of his life. Fred tried to reassure Dutch, but Dutch knew better; he could feel the pain.

As others approached, they kept several feet away as in shock. Fred yelled, "Call 911!"

"But that's the hospital, not the vet."

"Call 911; this is Dutch, not just any animal."

It seemed like forever before the ambulance arrived. Fred tore his shirt and tied it around Dutch's legs and chest to keep him from bleeding to death before the medics got there. Two medics got out of the ambulance and started to attend to Dutch. They could see the concern on everyone's face and had heard of Dutch and how special he was. The ambulance couldn't get close enough to Dutch, so they pulled out the stretcher and gently rolled him onto it. The driver had already called the hospital emergency room and requested OR to stand by. He then called the vet's office and asked to have him get to the hospital as soon as possible. He also requested blood, he didn't exactly know what the vet would do, but the vet had to have something he used for surgeries. The vet knew Dutch well and he was only too happy to help, even though it meant he had to reschedule the day's patients. Fred insisted on riding in the back with Dutch. Everyone knew how Fred was all gruff talk but loved Dutch immensely.

After the ambulance left, just as the Professor headed toward the administration building, he heard a call from one of the officers about 50 feet away.

"Hey, over here guys!"

The logical question on everyone's mind was "What did you find?"

Nothing was said; people just surrounded the officer who knelt down examining a huge dead mountain lion. Then the officers spoke, "I saw this cat on TV last night. It's the one that is a little crazy and has left his natural home and been a real problem for the city. He ran out of food and started getting into the garbage cans. He hurt a little boy last week; that's why he was on the news. He looks real sick. The little dog is lucky he didn't get caught by this cougar, he's about the size of the cougar's lunch."

"Well, he won't be hurting any more little kids; Dutch took care of him. He's a real hero." Everyone started to leave again. The officers said they would be back later to get the cat, but they needed to find out if the vet needed to do any testing on the carcass. What was on the Professor's mind was "Who's going to tell Robin about Dutch."

Chewie started back too, not understanding all that had happened, but he knew Dutch was in trouble and now the responsibility of security at "THE YARD" was his. He was way too young for this, although he had been the one to keep the other puppies in line. He would have to rise to the responsibility. From now on he would patrol just as he had been taught by Dutch.

Robin came by "THE YARD" as quickly as she could when she heard the news. The first thing out of her mouth as she entered the admin building was, "Have you heard how Dutch is doing?"

The Professor had waited for her. He really wanted to be at the hospital with Fred, but knew he needed to be with Robin. "Nothing yet, Fred is still at the hospital. He said he would call if Dutch didn't make it."

"It's really bad - huh? Do you think it's alright to pray for a dog?"

"The Bible says to pray about all things, it couldn't hurt."

Robin was surprised that the Professor even knew what the Bible was, but he was right. Praying was something she could do, and only God controls life and death anyway. Robin wished she could go cry in Josh's arms, but she hadn't heard from him either. Now Princess became more valuable in her mind. She would take her home tonight and ask if her parents she could stay.

About an hour later the call came, Dutch had lost so much blood but if he lived through the night, he might make it. Robin started for home then turned to the Professor, "Do you think we should change the name of Chewie to Dutch Jr.?"

"Yes child, I think he earned it. I'll tell Fred when he returns; you'd better tell Chewie on your way out. He has a big reputation to live up to, but he also has a good start."

Robin started home with Princess and her thoughts were mixed. Dutch was on her mind and she needed to find the right words to try to get her parents to accept Princess as a member of the family. She and Princess reached the house early and her dad heard her come in. "Robin, come in here for a minute." That rarely happened - her dad looking for her. "What's up Dad?" She tried to be very upbeat for Princess's sake, but her heart was sad for Dutch. Her dad spotted the dog in her arms as soon as she entered the room. Robin thought, "Curtains! It's already over, the cats out of the bag."

"Come over here," her dad said gently. "I suppose this is one of Dutch's pups." One of Dutch's pups? Robin didn't even think her dad was aware of Dutch, or "THE YARD." "Yes Dad, it's the last one of the litter. I was hoping you would let me keep her; she would even be good for you and Mom to have around for company. How do you know about Dutch?"

"Actually, it's news all over the city. It's even on the evening news. Dutch is quite the hero, and his pups will really be in demand after all this publicity. The dog can stay for now until we can talk this thing out. We wouldn't have any trouble finding another home for her now if we decide not to keep her. I just don't want her to be the only dog at "THE YARD," other than the watch dog of course." Then he paused for a second and starred at the dog. This is probably the longest conversation they had in years. Then he said, "It's too bad about Dutch, he was a legend long ago when he was a real crime fighter. He was the best dog the department ever had. They thought they would retire him to "THE YARD," but I guess you couldn't keep him from working. I thought he would keep the Professor company in his old age, but I guess that job was tougher than being the dog of "THE YARD." They both smiled and Robin went to give Mom the news. Things would be different with her parents being older and adding a young pup to the mix. It was nice that she would be a family dog, she could add love and excitement for the whole family and they could share the responsibility.

Chapter 13

The night was quiet and most got a well-deserved good night's sleep. It was in the wee hours of the morning that Dutch slipped away. By the time the nurses noticed he was not breathing or making any sounds; he was gone. The nurses decided not to notify anyone other than Fred, who was sleeping in the waiting room. Fred was glad Dutch's pain was gone, but he would miss him more than he ever expected. Visions of the past flew through his mind.

When Dutch was young, his personality was almost human. Fred remembered when he first saw him, or was it when Dutch first saw Fred? Fred was employed as a rookie police officer and he had been given the assignment of obtaining an auto accident report. It was common practice to leave the vehicles involved in the accident in the middle of the road until the police could examine their resting position, the damage and tire tracks. Fred was in the middle of the road when a speeding car came out of nowhere and headed right for him. The next thing that Fred knew, he was clear of the speeding car and lying on the side of the road.

He was told later that a large German shepherd had knocked him out of the way and then ran off as fast as he had arrived. Fred hunted for that dog for days until he found him living on his own a few blocks away in a vacant field. He had been abandoned. Fred was told by the locals that the dog lived off the food he could find or beg for. He looked a mess; dirty, mangy and under-nourished. Fred took the dog home and tried to clean him up. It was going to take several tries before the word clean could even be used. His idea was to try to get him into his Sergeant's heart and maybe be able to live at the station and be trained for police work. Fred thought he would have a better chance if he tried to anticipate any objections the Sergeant would come up with. Two things came to mind; where did the dog come from and was he in good physical and mental condition? Fred looked through all the missing animal reports and made an appointment with the vet for the next morning before his shift.

"Fred, this dog is dirty and under fed, but in pretty good condition otherwise."

"Glad to hear that, any idea about how old he is?"

"Actually, he's about four from what I can tell. I think he has a micro-chip ID, but my reader is on the blink. In a couple of days we could have a lot more information about him," replied the vet. "I'll just hold him here for a few days and clean him up and see if I can get my reader to work. I'll call you when I get something."

Fred thanked the vet and went to work, hoping the call would be soon. He was starting to like the idea of having the dog for company since he had no one else at home. Besides, the dog may have saved his life. Strange thoughts went through his mind, like did the dog mean to push him out of the way of the car or was it just a coincidence? Thoughts went through his mind all day during his routine shift. The vet hadn't called yet, although it had been only eight hours, much less than a few days. With nothing to lose, Fred dropped by the vets on the way home. The vet was just finishing up his day but heard the bell of the entry door, looked out and saw Fred. He was ready to go home, but didn't want to offend Fred either.

"Be with you in a minute Fred. I just want to check the exam rooms. I think your dog likes it here; at least he enjoyed his supper."

His dog! That sounded good to Fred. "Anything new, I mean did you get any information yet?"

"As a matter of fact I did. My reader started working after the fourth kick, so I was able to track down the owners. It was easy. That dog is registered as a show dog with a champion line."

Fred heart sank, "I guess that eliminates the possibility of him staying with me".

"Actually, he has a royal blood line, and his name is Dutch."

"You can't tell that from looking at him now."

"No, but he has good lines and in time maybe he can return to the form his parents had."

"Did you find the owner yet?"

"Well, that's where it gets interesting. The dog was purchased sight unseen by a breeder. He was being shipped cross country about a year ago when the dog broke loose from the crate. They had given the dog up and had accepted an insurance settlement. Now that he's found, it could get complicated. The owner would like to give up all claims on the dog if you can clear it with the insurance company."

Then the thought came to Fred, "If I can sell the sergeant on Dutch for the first K9 unit, he can make the call to the insurance company. He has a way with people." And that's just what he did. Not even the insurance company wanted to mess with his sergeant, and now he could train Dutch for police duties.

It took a lot of time and a few training courses, but after a few months Fred and Dutch became inseparable and quite a team. Since the station had no provisions for a dog, Fred took him home every night. Dutch was eager to please; he had never known a companion before. In addition, the department had a new resource to help in their activities. Dutch was over worked, if anything. He sure made a name for himself and he didn't hurt Fred's reputation either.

They worked together for almost ten years, when Fred was offered the job of keeper of "THE YARD. Fred moved into the admin building along with several other special duty officers, Dutch, and one old detective that the department didn't have the heart to retire. It was Professor Klueless. Dutch was involved in many of the Professor's important cases. The Professor was really sharp in his day too, but just as he was approaching retirement his mind took a turn for the worse. Some thought it was too many hours on the job. Some thought it was all the junk food he ate. He was well known in every coffee and donut shop in the city. Over the next couple of years "THE YARD" deteriorated for lack of city funds; the tax payers didn't want their money to be spent on land-scaping. To the entire city, the old estate became known as "THE YARD."

When Fred got back to "THE YARD" the first one to tell the news to was the Professor. It was hard to tell how the Professor was taking it; he was returning to his usual blank stare at the wall. With all the success and enthusiasm he had lately, it was hard to see him get back to his old routine. Next would be harder, telling Robin. Even though it wasn't even lunch time, Fred felt that he needed to make contact with Robin. He signed out, drove over to the school and went into the principal's office to have Robin called from class. As Robin went to the principal's office, she caught a glimpse of big bertha and broke out in tears. By the time she got to Fred, what she needed most was a dry shoulder to cry on. No words were spoken, none had to be. After a time, both Fred and Robin left. Neither had a dry eye.

Chapter 14

Robin had enough excitement in her life for a while; some good, some not so good. At least during the last few months, she had begun to be better friends with Fred and Professor Klueless. She returned to her normal schedule of meeting Dutch Jr., waving to Fred and taking a seat in the Professor's office. Professor Klueless was clueless about most of the things around him. He started to open up to Robin a little, talking about how great it was for him to be useful again around "THE YARD." He even started to reminisce about the old days and cases that would make your hair stand on end. Without warning, Fred slammed the door open with a note and handed it to Robin. "For me?" Fred nodded and left as Robin's heart began to pound. "Now what?" she thought. She unfolded the note and read, "Sorry I left so suddenly, a lot has happened. I will explain later. Josh"

Now her heart was really pounding. She had missed him so much and during all that had happened she couldn't share any of it with him. She loved him so much, but how could he leave without a word, and why didn't he at least call her to explain? She was going from love to anger as her mind played tricks on her with crazy explanations. Besides, why didn't he call her at home where she could talk? Why did she have to get a note from the police? Now she was really getting super charged.

The Professor continued to reminisce, but Robin didn't hear anything more that he said. Finally, she just got up and started home. Her eyes filled with tears for Josh and then she became red with anger as she began to kick everything in her path. She was confused, somewhere between love and anger. The stupid music the Professor played in his office sometimes went through her mind, "You always hurt the one you love, the one you shouldn't hurt at all." All she had ever wanted was someone to love her and need her. She would have forgiven Josh for anything when he was here, but now she wasn't so sure. She burst though the back door right past her Mom and headed upstairs, slamming the door behind her. Thoughts went through her mother's mind too, but she took the easy way out and thought that whatever it was, now was not the time for talking.

Robin didn't even come down for supper. She just lay on her bed, hugging Princess and crying. Whether they were tears of despair or anger, she wasn't sure. Her Mom waited until after the dishes were done before she went up to Robin's room with a warmed plate of beef stew. "What's wrong Honey, can you talk about it?"

Robin didn't know how to talk with her Mom about personal issues; she always kept things to herself. She needed to let things out or she would bust. "Mom, it's Josh! I love him so much and he left me without a word. How could he do that to me, after all we meant to each other?"

"Maybe he couldn't help it," her Mom replied.

"He could have contacted me somehow, if he had really wanted too."

"Don't judge him too harshly until you have heard the whole story."

"I don't know if I want to hear the whole story? How could he do this to me?"

It was hard for Robin to try to grow up so fast. Robin really loved Josh, but was hurt so badly that she couldn't be logical about him. She was just acting like a woman, "Pure emotion," her Mom thought." Then she thought, "Oh boy what am I thinking? This is the real thing, but it seems like yesterday I was just rocking her to sleep in my arms."

"Robin, I know things are hard for you right now, but remember what the Bible says; we must wait on the Lord. Wait honey, although it is the hardest thing you may ever do."

"I hope I never see Josh again!"

Her Mom could see that she could be of no use right now, so she hugged Robin and went downstairs. Robin grabbed Princess and squeezed maybe a little too tight and cried herself to sleep.

The next few days, Robin went through her normal routines again, but her mind was never off of Josh. Josh had called Robin at home several times, but either she was gone or she refused to talk to him. She was going to show him that she could learn to get along without him. After all, he wasn't worthy of her friendship. Friends don't abandon friends.

As Robin went to "THE YARD" the next day, she closed herself up with the Professor and acted as if she was listening to him ramble on. It made the

Professor happy just to have somebody around. They needed to talk about the upcoming holiday parade since both of them were asked to be in one of the lead cars. Even Dutch Jr. was invited. "Holiday parades aren't what they used to be," the Professor said, "especially in a winter climate, but I guess that depends on how young at heart you are."

Josh finally felt as if the world was being straightened out. He called his grandfather and asked for his clothes to be shipped to Arizona. His dad had already leased a town home about 10 minutes away from the stadium. Josh was to start college the next fall, but he could have the whole first part of the year to get acclimated to his dad, warm weather and a new life style. He was very excited about everything - everything except Robin. He wondered why she wouldn't even talk to him. She should be happy for him. He had heard the news of her adventures; she should be on cloud nine, too. If only he could talk to her. Well, calling wasn't going to do it. He had an idea. He would put his dad on the spot for the first time in his life.

That night when his dad came home, Josh cornered him with what he thought was a great idea.

"Dad, I hope you had a good day at work?" Josh smiled.

His dad was not around enough to understand kids, but he knew when he was being set up. "Everything was great Josh; I hope you had a good day too. Shall we go out for supper tonight, how about a steak and then some bowling?"

"Sounds great, but I have a favor to ask you."

"I would have never guessed, but I owe you a few. What do you have in mind?"

"Do you regularly get a limo?"

"Well, yes Son. The team has a contract with a world-wide company. Why? You're not planning on taking one all the way back to Robin, are you?"

Josh could see that his dad was smarter that he thought, not being around kids and all.

"No, but I would like to rent one; a big white one." The two of them discussed Josh's plan. Finally, his dad said, "It's ok with me, but you had better call Grandpa and get it worked out on his end."

Josh just smiled. He was in love with his idea and was getting excited about seeing Robin again.

Chapter 15

It was Saturday morning and the day of the big parade. The Professor and Robin were to ride in the lead cars and had their choice of a convertible or big bertha. It was a little chilly, but they opted for the convertible anyway. A car was to pick Robin up early so she could prepare for her experience. Promptly at 9 a.m. a big white limo parked in front of the house. No one came out so Robin assumed that she should just go down and talk to the driver. She grabbed her stuff, gave her Mom a hug and ran out the door. The car was really big. She wondered how many people were in it, but she couldn't see through the dark windows. She decided since it probably had others already inside, to just open the large passenger door and introduce herself. She opened the door, and felt faint. It was Josh, alone in the car!

"What are you doing here? I thought you were in Arizona."

"And miss one of the biggest days in my best girl's life?"

Robin didn't know what to say, she had tried to reconcile herself to never seeing Josh again. Her anger had been so intense that she hadn't had a normal thought in months. Now Josh was here and she was speechless. He motioned for her not to say a word, just enter the car and give him the usual hug. She got in, and gave him their usual hug. Now they both were sure this would be forever. She snuggled in his arms as the car drove off to the starting position at the parade. Slowly, Robin and Josh began to open up and catch up on the last few months. Robin's anger and hurt feelings about Josh not telling her before he left didn't seem important anymore. Josh thought it was kind of like when we get to heaven; the things of earth will grow strangely dim in the light of His glory and grace.

Josh found a place on the route to watch the parade and Robin, the Professor and Dutch Jr. took their place of honor in the back seat of a vintage convertible. It was a three mile route and people cheered so loudly that Dutch began to softly howl, or was it singing? When the parade was over, all were exhausted. Dutch Jr. was so happy to get back to work he took off at a dead run as if he had to make up for the time he missed. The Professor and Fred poured a cup of coffee and began to talk about the good old days. Robin, she went to Josh's grandfather's house and stayed for dinner. There was a lot to talk about, but it was about the future, not the past.

Josh stayed in town for several weeks; Christmas was coming and his dad wanted to spend the time with his family, cold weather or not. The future never looked brighter. Dutch Jr. had a real home with great responsibility, the Professor was useful one more time and Josh would go to school in Arizona. Robin? She would attend the same school as Josh in Arizona and stay on campus. Christmas may be cold, but the summer would be hot.

Things worked out for several months with Josh and Robin in Arizona. Robin even learned to open up to others, now that her fears of being useless were over; Josh saw to that. As Robin was sitting in her first hour class waiting for the day to begin, the college professor handed her a note. It was from Fred. "Robin, the Professor was involved in a traffic accident. I am at the hospital now, but he is unconscious. When I was out to lunch he got another one of his ideas on a case, grabbed the keys and tried to drive somewhere. He was hit in the driver's door as he went through a red light. I'll send you more information as it unfolds, Love Fred."

Robin thought for a moment, "Love Fred." She now had the love of a large family, one like she had always wanted. She remembered how it was with Dutch when he needed her. She couldn't let her family down. She ran out of the room to make plans to return to "THE YARD." Hopefully, Josh would go with her.

CPSIA information can be obtained at www.ICGtesting.com
Printed in the USA
BVOW02s0551040216

435322BV00001B/17/P